Praise for *Oliver's Surprise*

"For the past forty years I have raced along the waters of Narragansett Bay. After reading *Oliver's Surprise* my vision of the area will be of the infamous hurricane of 1938 and of the young Oliver seeing the catastrophe take place."

–Gary Jobson, ESPN commentator
and America's Cup Hall of Fame member

"The best historical fiction combines good research with good storytelling, and *Oliver's Surprise* has it all. Carol Newman Cronin writes with authority about the sea and her home in Rhode Island, and her thorough investigation of the Hurricane of '38 shines through. Chock full of adventure, history, sailing, time travel, a likeable protagonist, *Oliver's Surprise* is about as much fun as you can have without actually being on board a boat!"

–James L. Nelson, author of the *Revolution at Sea Saga* and *George Washington's Secret Navy*

"A vivid glimpse of boatyard life for a modern boy whisked back to his grandfather's day, just before the Hurricane of '38."

–Molly Banc
When

"A boy, a boat, and a bump on the head were all the elements needed...the nautical tale is a treasure chest of surprises."

–*The Jamestown Press*

"For a kid smitten with the sea, an old schooner is the ideal vehicle for going back in time. Through young Oliver's eyes, Carol Newman Cronin offers a view of life along the 1930's Jamestown waterfront, just before the storm changed it forever. Above all, *Oliver's Surprise* reminds us of the connectedness of family and friends through generations."

–John Burnham, Editorial Director at Boats.com

"I sat down to read *Oliver's Surprise* in California and was immediately transported to Jamestown and Narragansett Bay. This charming story—with lovely illustrations—captures two different eras in a very special place."

–Pease Glaser, *Olympic Silver Medalist*

"*Oliver's Surprise* is a wonderful young adult adventure story. The writing is fast-paced and filled with strong verbs and nautical terms. It reminds me of the *Wizard of Oz*, *Back to the Future*, and *Tom Sawyer*, and *Huckleberry Finn* all rolled into one. Well done!"

-Paula Margulies, author of *Coyote Heart*

"When our children were toddling, my wife's wish for them was confidence. But as they grew into teens what she wanted most for them was perspective. *Oliver's Surprise* is a fetching tale about a kid who through an uncommon set of travels gains just that kind of perspective—the kind that opens a curiosity about our own origins, the kind that places values from the past in our contemporary life, the kind that steers us toward our better selves. All this, and schooners, too."

–Tim Murphy, Editor-at-Large
of *Cruising World*

"...an engaging tale woven by one of sailing's modern-day racing stars...a pleasant time-travel adventure for all ages."

–Elaine Dickinson, Managing Editor
of *BoatUS Magazine*

OLIVER'S SURPRISE

OLIVER'S SURPRISE

A Boy, A Schooner, and the Great Hurricane of 1938

REVISED

CAROL NEWMAN CRONIN

ILLUSTRATED BY
LAURIE ANN CRONIN

GEMMA

Boston

First published by GemmaMedia in 2009.

GemmaMedia
230 Commercial Street
Boston MA 02109 USA
617 938 9833
www.gemmamedia.com

Printed in the United States of America

12   11   10   09   1   2   3   4   5

ISBN: 978-1-934848-62-3

Library of Congress Preassigned Control Number (PCN) applied for

Cover photo by Onne van der Wal.
www.vanderwal.com

Book design by Live Wire.
www.livewirepress.com

to Paul
who had the idea

and

to Oliver
who was the inspiration

Contents

Sea-Fever

I must go down to the seas again, to the lonely sea and the sky,
And all I ask is a tall ship and a star to steer her by,
And the wheel's kick and the wind's song and the white sail's
*   shaking,*
And a gray mist on the sea's face, and a gray dawn breaking.

I must go down to the seas again, for the call of the running tide
Is a wild call and a clear call that may not be denied;
And all I ask is a windy day with the white clouds flying,
And the flung spray and the blown spume, and the sea-gulls
crying.

I must go down to the seas again, to the vagrant gypsy life,
To the gull's way and the whale's way, where the wind's like
*   a whetted knife;*
And all I ask is a merry yarn from a laughing fellow-rover,
And quiet sleep and a sweet dream when the long trick's over.

– John Masefield

from <u>Poems by John Masefield</u>, Macmillan, 1938.

Map of Jamestown

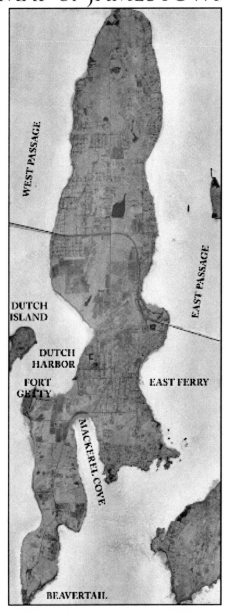

WEST PASSAGE

EAST PASSAGE

DUTCH
ISLAND

DUTCH
HARBOR

FORT
GETTY

EAST FERRY

MACKEREL COVE

BEAVERTAIL

His mother was gonna be mad.

One o'clock on a Thursday afternoon and Oliver was rowing out across the quiet harbor. All Mom had to do was glance up and she'd see him, shaggy dark head above white skiff, creeping away from the shoreline. Luckily she was totally focused on hauling a boat out of the water with her new hydraulic trailer. That's why he'd been able to scramble unseen down to the rocks, unclip Sparky, and be free.

It was just too nice a day to waste inside learning about some hurricane that happened a gazillion years ago. Who'd decided school should start in September, anyway? The sunshine warming the back of his neck still felt like summer.

He hadn't planned on skipping out of school when he thumped out the cafeteria door. His feet just started running, pizza jiggling in his belly, across the baseball and soccer fields and into the woods, down through the neighbors' yards, until he fetched up behind the yellow boatyard shed. Once he could see Sparky gleaming in the September sunshine, his breathing steadied and the lonely ache inside him felt almost bearable again.

Grampa had died in his sleep last July, two days before his hundredth birthday. He'd never liked big parties so maybe that was his way out. There were so many questions Oliver had never asked, about the boatyard and Sparky and Grandma Nellie. And now that it was too late, the only place he felt close to Grampa was on the harbor they both loved.

Grampa's name had been Oliver too, and he'd left school for good at thirteen to go fishing. When a trawl dropped on his foot and smashed three of his toes, he bought the property next to the ferry dock and started a boatyard.

Sixty years later, he passed the business down to Oliver's mom and settled into the rocker on the front porch of the house. Every day after school last spring, Oliver would run up the steps and lean into him. His tan workshirt always smelled like sawdust.

"Whatcha doing, Grampa?" Oliver'd ask.

"Whistling and whittling," Grampa would reply, his smile stretching across wrinkled cheeks. Wrapping an arm around Oliver, he'd pull him in close to show off the lifelike duck or seal he'd carved. Oliver had a whole collection of Grampa's animals on a special shelf by his bed. They were way better than those stupid Bionicles his younger brother liked to build.

Slicing varnished oars into the water, Oliver braced his sneakers to lean into each stroke like he'd been taught. He was supposed to tell someone when he went rowing, but today following the rules would just get him sent back to recess. And rowing was a lot more fun than trying to make a soccer ball go where he wanted.

He hadn't been paying much attention to where he was going, but when Sparky's fender bumped up against the towering topsides of Surprise, he shipped the oars and stowed them under the thwart. The schooner's owner, Cap'n Eli, was in the hospital and wouldn't mind Oliver hiding out in the cockpit. Maybe he could even catch a bluefish. Bringing home dinner would make it easier to face his mother, once the school called.

He peeled off his socks and sneakers and dropped them on the stern thwart alongside his backpack and sweatshirt. Cap'n Eli always said there were plenty of ways for a boat to get dirty without bringing shore muck aboard. Climbing up the black bulwark, Oliver could almost see the old man sitting in the cockpit, wispy white hair standing up from his head. Even with old puffed-up knuckles he could still manage the chisels and scrapers that filled up his tired toolbox, and he'd been scraping paint the last time Oliver had rowed out to visit. "Making the old girl shipshape again," he'd said, one pale blue eye closing into a wink. A thick edge of tan ran just inboard of the coaming, so he hadn't quite finished stripping the cockpit seat before that blood vessel stroked his brain.

Oliver loved listening to Cap'n Eli's stories about the cargoes he'd carried on Surprise. Bricks and lumber down the Bay, oysters and fish back up to Providence. When Grampa cleaned out his office he'd found a grainy photo of Surprise sailing up West Passage under her four lowers: mainsail, foresail, jumbo, and jib. Grampa said the black schooner was the finest coaster of her day, back before all the bridges and highways, when sail was still the best way to get around and knowing the currents meant a faster delivery and a better price.

Nowadays her decking had dried out and cracked, and the mainsail peeked white through a rotten sailcover. But Oliver could still feel her power, and the schooner tugged at her mooring in the gentle swell as if she was eager to get underway again. Grabbing the wheel in one hand and bristly mainsheet in the other, he imagined the deck heeling underfoot and huge sails billowing overhead as he steered a cargo of lobsters up the Bay.

The rumbling growl of a diesel pulled his gaze back toward the boatyard. Mom was backing the shiny trailer into the storage shed,

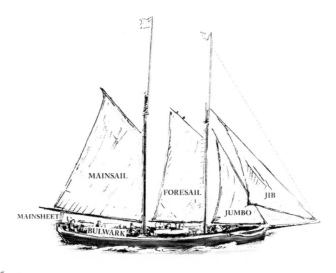

a large sailboat held between its mittened pads. She'd set it down on blocking, support it with boat stands, and then slither the trailer out and head back to the ramp for the next boat.

When she came out of the huge shed, she'd be sure to check over the harbor. If she spotted white Sparky against the black topsides of Surprise, her left eyebrow would arch up like the crayon waves he used to draw and she'd storm out to Surprise in the workboat to drag him back to school. Better make sure to move the skiff to the starboard side, once the seabreeze built enough to swing the schooner around to the south.

Dutch Island looked so much closer from here. The furry outline separated into trees, brambles, and the square crumble of abandoned lighthouse. South of the island, on the other side of the channel out to West Passage, shiny RV's covered the grassy knoll at Fort Getty's trailer park. When Oliver rode his bike over there he couldn't believe all the flower gardens and the signs people had put up. "The Wilsons," and "Welcome to the Turners' House." As if it was a regular neighborhood, not one that drove away every October.

His own house was out of sight, just up the hill behind the big yellow shed. His favorite playground was the boatyard, and the town pier that stuck out into the harbor. Squinting, he tried to picture the white tongue of dock surrounded by workboats like Surprise and Sparky, instead of row after row of shiny yachts stamped out of fiberglass and plastic.

Cap'n Eli had been Grampa's best friend, so he could've told Oliver more about the old days if he hadn't gotten so sick. Dad didn't think Eli would ever climb aboard Surprise again. And Mom said when Eli died she'd probably just haul the schooner out of the water. Nobody wanted a tired old coaster anymore, no matter how awesome she was in her day.

A puff of seabreeze darted across the water, its salty bite raising goosebumps on his bare legs and arms. He'd never been down below on Surprise before, but Cap'n Eli wouldn't mind him keeping warm in the cabin until the bluefish started slapping. Creeping forward, he pushed all his weight against the sticky companionway hatch and managed to slide it open halfway, releasing a whiff of old wood that reminded him of Grampa. He couldn't see down into the gloom when he felt for the ladder—so his bare feet slipped past the top step. Before he could grab onto anything, he tumbled six feet down onto the cabin sole, whacking his head on something sharp. The last thing he saw was a large cloud scudding across the blue sky high overhead, far above the open hatch.

ↅ   ↅ   ↅ   ↅ   ↅ

The cloud had disappeared by the time Oliver woke up. Sitting up too fast started his head spinning, so he lay back down again.

Voices outside and a thunk against the bottom of the hull—that's what had brought him awake. Could Surprise have dragged her mooring up onto the beach? The wind had been light and the tide just starting to ebb when he fell, but how long ago was that?

His head throbbed, and his fingers found— ouch—a lump that matched the broomstick handle of a wooden carryall. What a stupid place for Cap'n Eli to leave his toolbox, right in the middle of the cabin. And most of the tools were missing, which would make him really mad.

Another thunk on the hull made Oliver sit up again, and this time his head stayed on his shoulders. He crept onto his knees and then to his feet, swallowing down pizza-flavored bile. What if someone had come to steal more tools off the old boat? Everyone knew Eli was sick. He lifted one foot to the bottom step of the ladder.

Surprise lurched forward, and he reached out a hand to brace himself against the engine.

Engine! What was that doing on board? "First thing I done when I bought this old girl was to heave the clunker over the side," Cap'n Eli had told him. "Makes a darn good mooring block." Now that clunker hunkered down on its mounts, shiny as his dad's new car.

Another lurch, and the bow was going up. As if they were on the ramp! Could his mom be hauling Surprise? That meant Eli had... Oliver scrambled up the ladder, the soft pads of his feet digging into each tread. Once he could see over the hatch coaming, the lump on the back of his head began to throb all over again.

Either side of Surprise an oak scaffold rose to boom height, cradling her hull as she crawled up onto the land. Spindly telephone poles marched up a treeless hill. The boatyard shed sprawled low, red, and tired. To his right, the town pier had darkened to oily sand, and a ferryboat as big as his house nosed between pilings at the end. A few unfamiliar catboats and one gaff-rigged yawl swung to the seabreeze, just off the boatyard dock, but the rest of the harbor was empty. Had he passed out right through hauling season? And where were all the trees?

And to his left—jeez! Where was the bridge? The concrete highway connecting his island to the mainland was gone. Nothing but blue water lapping at green fields, all the way up Narragansett Bay. He crawled out into the cockpit and stood up, gingerly touching the lump on his head.

"You boy!" A voice bellowed from the ground. "Get down from there!"

Now he would be sent back to recess, just when things were getting really cool. Sighing, he started toward the bow so he could climb down onto the hydraulic trailer. But no metal platform arched up in welcome. Instead a rusty engine belched thick smoke, next to a drum wound in cable as thick as Oliver's arm.

"Not that way!" the voice hollered. "Off the port side. Look lively now!"

Oliver scurried back to the widest part of the boat, where the large wooden structure loomed closest to the deck. As he swung a bare foot over the lifeline and scrambled down the frame, it felt like he was leaving the only friend he had in this strange new world.

"How'd you get up there?"

Oliver stared up at the man. Dark crewcut, and tan shirtsleeves rolled up onto muscled forearms. Except for a shot of gray on his left temple, the guy could be a stunt double for Uncle Matthew.

"Whatcha looking at?" this not quite stranger demanded. "And how'd you get aboard Cap'n Sam's boat? You stowaway up in Providence?"

"That's Surprise," Oliver said. Though she looked kind of—new. "Isn't it?"

"Isn't it, sir," the man corrected. "You're not out of short pants yet, you call me sir. Even if your short pants was built for someone taller." Eyes traveled down Oliver's cargo shorts to where bare calves emerged.

"Yes, ah, sir." Oliver resisted the urge to salute by sliding his hands into his pockets.

"And take those greasy mitts out where I can see 'em! What's your name?"

"Oliver."

"Sir," he repeated. "Who taught you manners?"

Oliver pressed his lips together. No point in dragging Mom into this.

"Huh. Maybe the same person who never takes you to the barber. How old are you?"

"Twelve. And a half. Sir."

"And what were you doing on Cap'n Sam's boat?"

"That is Surprise, isn't it? Sir?"

"Course that's Surprise. Only schooner in Dutch Harbor. You telling me you're the surprise?" One corner of the narrow mouth lifted, settling Oliver's stomach just a little.

Oliver shook his head. "It's just that I'm wondering what happened to Cap'n Eli, sir. If you say she belongs to Cap'n Sam now."

Thick eyebrows merged above blue eyes. "Never heard of your Cap'n Eli. Cap'n Sam's owned her since she came off the ways." His eyebrows lowered even further. "You're not from around here, are you lad?"

Before Oliver could answer, a shout dragged his questioner's attention back toward the schooner. Oliver glanced around again, looking for something, anything, to explain what had happened to him.

A parade of black cars kicked up a cloud of dust as they bumped down the pier to line up for the ferry. Either side of the road, people walked down the hill. Most carried boxes, and all of them, men and women, wore hats right out of an old movie. Three skiffs that looked just like Sparky clustered around the yard dock.

He recognized the shape of the shoreline and his questioner had said this was Dutch Harbor, so he knew where he was. He just wasn't exactly sure about the *when*.

"Oliver, was it?"

The man's eyes flicked back to him.

"Yes, sir."

"A fine name." He smiled. "And your family name?"

"You mean my last name?"

"Answer the question, boy."

"Nichols-Bee, sir."

"Nicklesby? Hmm. I don't recall anybody from up the Bay by that name. But you can't be all bad, if you're a Red Sox fan." He pointed to Oliver's chest. "That's quite a fancy shirt you've got."

"Yes, sir." Oliver glanced down at the red embroidery. "It's my favorite."

"Well it's too bad I can't spare the time to sail you back up to Providence. The seabreeze is perfect." He turned toward the shed. "Mason!"

"Yes, Mr. Oliver?" The round man was carrying what looked like a long-handled hoe.

"You say you needed another pair of hands?"

"Sure thing, boss."

The dark-haired man turned back to him.

"Might as well put you to work until someone comes looking for you. Mason'll show you what to do." And turning on his heel, the Uncle Matthew look-alike headed up toward the yard office.

The roll and hitch to his gait, as if he were missing three toes on his left foot! He had to be imitating his grandfather, like Mom's foreman used to do just after Grampa retired. But how would this guy know Grampa? He'd bought the yard during the Depression. And that was—

"Ow!" Something thumped against the back of his head, dangerously close to the tender lump.

"Quit your daydreamin', boy," the man called Mason growled.

Not knowing what else to do, Oliver followed Mason's duck-like waddle back toward Surprise. Dripping from every seam, the boat's underbody was dark and furry with seaweed. Someone should pressure-wash her before the growth dried and stuck to her planking so hard it would have to be sanded off. Mom's foreman had let Oliver use the pressure washer once to clean Sparky's bottom, and the high-pressure jet got the job done fast. It was the only tool for cleaning off thick muck like this, even if it was as squirmy and hard to handle as a firehose.

Mason handed him a large piece of burlap and the hoe.

"What's this?"

"Never scraped a bottom before?" Mason scowled. "I always get stuck with the lubbers." Tying the fabric over the flat metal, he swiped it against the keel, leaving behind a clean stripe of green bottom paint. "See? Get all the growth off quick, before it dries. And don't be digging out any caulking or Mr. Nichols'll have your hide."

Mr. Nichols—Mr. Oliver Nichols! His grandfather's name.

Oliver scraped at the fuzzy growth clinging to the keel, trying not to breathe in the stench. A glob of brown freed by the hoe landed on his sleeve, and his bare arms quickly speckled with slime. Good thing he'd left his school sweatshirt on Sparky. Where was Sparky, anyway? He could sure use his sneakers, now that large gravel chunks dug into his feet. Though Mason wasn't wearing shoes. Hearing the clunk and scrape start up on the far side of the hull, Oliver lifted his heavy tool again, trying not to grimace.

He'd cleaned the worst of the slime off the long keel and was looking up at the waterline high overhead when Mason reappeared with a small stepladder. "You might need this."

"Thanks, Mason! I mean, sir." Digging the four legs into the gravel, Oliver climbed to the top step. The waterline had the thickest growth, proving that not everything was different in this strange world.

Arms burning from holding the heavy tool over his head, he rested the wooden handle on the ground to gaze across the not quite familiar harbor. It looked so empty without all the moored boats, and Dutch Island's lighthouse stood square and white and proud at the entrance. Fort Getty's shiny RV's had been replaced by a lone American flag fluttering above a green field. And the northern Bay seemed impossibly wide without the bridge.

The ferry had crossed the harbor and tied

19

up to a dock on the near side of Dutch Island, where antlike men paraded down the hill to meet it. Grampa had told his little brother Nat endless stories about the soldiers who trained on the island between the two big wars. So World War II hadn't happened yet, which meant neither had Vietnam or Iraq. Mason had probably never heard of either place.

"Whatcha lookin at, boy?" Mason reappeared, swinging his slimy hoe toward Oliver's backside. "At this rate it'll take you till sunset tomorrow to finish."

Oliver dragged his attention back to a stubborn piece of seaweed clinging to Surprise. The old girl had sure seen a lot of changes in her lifetime. If only she could tell him what to do next.

He didn't climb off the ladder until just before sunset, his arms aching. Mom would really be mad now, and worried too. He was supposed to be home before dark no matter what. And even though he could see his house right up the street, he couldn't let her know he was okay if she hadn't been born yet. Stomach knotted tight, he followed Mason up the hill.

A large pump stood in front of the office, and Mason raised the handle to wash his hands. Oliver copied him, wiping the worst of the slime off his arms. Four chilly pumps later, he still smelled like low tide and his T-shirt stuck damp against his skin. What he needed was a nice hot shower and his sweatshirt. Shivering a little, he air-dried his hands, watching Mason and the other three workers amble up the road.

∽ ∽ ∽ ∽ ∽

After the men disappeared over the top of the hill, the man they called Mr. Oliver emerged from the office.

"You don't have a home tonight, do you son. How about you come upstairs with me? Nellie'll be happy to look after you."

"Nellie?"

"My wife. We haven't been blessed with children."

Grandma Nellie had died way back before Oliver's parents were even married. Grampa'd always talked about joining her in heaven like she was just away on a trip, and his eyes lit up just like now. But they'd had six kids! Gut clenching, Oliver followed the familiar roll-and-tip gait through the office door and up the steep wooden staircase. Had he already screwed up his own time, just by falling down Surprise's companionway?

Grampa stopped at the top of the steps in front of a paper calendar and pulled a pencil from behind his ear to X out another day. At the top it said 1938, like that was perfectly normal. And it was still September 14, but a Wednesday. Better look up the date on Mom's computer when he got home, to see if that made sense.

A meaty aroma greeted them inside a small room that didn't look anything like the tricked-out apartment his mom rented for big bucks in the summer. This ceiling was low, and two tiny windows filled with the red sunset. He could see all the way across the empty harbor, since there were no trees and no yellow boatyard shed in the way.

The closed doors beyond the stairs were familiar. In the apartment he knew, they led to a bedroom and a bathroom. Did bathrooms exist yet, or would he have to figure out how to flush an outhouse?

"What smells so good, Nellie Bell?" her husband bellowed. And Oliver knew then, for sure. Somehow he'd stepped back in time, and this unwrinkled man was his grandfather. He'd heard that bellow and that nickname too many times not to recognize both.

The woman smiled over her shoulder. "I made us some stew." Then she caught sight of Oliver, and her left eyebrow crested into a wave so exactly like his mom's he had to stop himself from racing into her arms.

"Where did you blow in from?" Setting a wooden spoon down on the stove, she smoothed the hair back out of his eyes.

"Young Oliver was on Surprise when we hauled her for painting," Grampa said. "Must've stowed away in Providence."

"Really!" Her eyebrow crested again. "First time I've heard of anyone pulling one over on Cap'n Sam. Maybe our new friend has a different story."

Had she spotted the family resemblance?

Nellie crossed to a tall wooden cabinet. "Well wherever you came from, young Oliver, it sure is nice to have a hungry boy to feed."

"Sit down, lad. Nellie will set your place."
Two woven placemats already lay on the table,
either side of a small pitcher of flowers.

Setting the table was his job at home, and
it felt strange not to help. Edging onto a stool,
he tried to remember his family history. Otis
was his grandfather's first child, nineteen years
older than Mom. She was born in 1958, which
meant Uncle O was born in, uh, 1939. So a
guy who was about to retire in Oliver's normal
world wouldn't even be alive until next year!
He hadn't messed up his family. Not yet, at
least.

Next to his favorite relative and across from
a grandmother he'd never met, Oliver's mind
overflowed with all the questions he'd thought
of since Grampa died. What was it like,
living through the Depression? Did it hurt a
lot losing three toes? Did it hurt more to lose
Nellie? She was a lot younger than Grampa, so
that must've been a real shock.

But he clamped his chapped lips together.
If he said the wrong thing, he might never be

born. Anyway Grampa always said that in his day, children were supposed to be seen and not heard.

"Shall we have grace?"

His grandfather reached out to take Oliver's hand. Oliver copied the bowed heads, trying not to grab onto Nellie's stove-warmed fingers too hard. They had this silence before dinner at home, too, when Dad got back from the hospital early enough and Mom wasn't hauling boats on the evening tide. Oliver always wondered when they could start eating, just like now.

After some private signal both adults squeezed and let go, smiling at each other. Nell ladled steaming stew into three bowls. "I'm so glad I made extra," she said. "I needed to use up the rabbit before it went bad."

Rabbit. Like Bunny, his old pet? Yuck. And nothing else on the table, except a plate of sliced beets. He stuck a spoon into the bowl and slurped, scorching his tongue.

"Careful, it's hot."

"Oh, yeah, thanks."

"Thank you, ma'am," his grandfather corrected.

"Thank you, ma'am," Oliver repeated.

Nellie's dark eyes sparkled. "What a lucky woman I am, to be seated at one table with two Olivers. But won't your family worry?"

"I run off a lot," Oliver mumbled around his next mouthful. The stew was really good.

"Why aren't you in school?"

"I left. Awhile ago." After lunch, in a different century.

"Good for you." Grampa nodded. "I did the same thing at your age. Schooling didn't make any difference once the banks went bust. I'd probably be bootlegging now if I hadn't gone fishing when I did. Instead I'm running my own business."

"Now Oliver." His grandma patted her husband's hand. "You know you never could've purchased the property if the bank hadn't taken it from Wiley. And don't be discouraging the boy from getting an education! I've heard you regret leaving school plenty of times when you were struggling to tot up a bill." She passed him the beets.

"You're right, Nell." Grampa shoveled three red slivers into his empty bowl. When Nellie offered them to Oliver, he shook his head, grimacing.

"But I sure know how the boy feels," Grampa said. "Hard to stay inside when the weather's as nice as today." He peered down his bony nose. "You must have an eye for quality to stow away on Surprise. She's the best coaster on the Bay."

"Yes, sir, I know."

Grandma Nell stood up to clear the empty bowls. Oliver'd been hoping for seconds, and he looked down to hide his disappointment. Then the oven door creaked open.

"A little birdie must've told me we'd have a guest tonight," she said. "I made a pie with those apples Mason brought."

"My favorite!" Grampa beamed. "Nothing better than a Nellie Bell apple pie."

She served them each a thick slice and a wedge of cheddar cheese. Cheese with pie? Copying his grandfather, Oliver broke off a chunk, put it in his mouth, and then chased it down with a large bite of steaming apples. Yum. He wiped his plate clean.

"Thank you, Nellie Bell. That was delicious." Grampa scraped back his chair. "Now, we'd better get a hold of your family, young Oliver. Do you know the phone number? I'll raise Beatrice and try to get a line off the island."

"Uh, well, you can't call 'em."

"They're not on the telephone?"

"You could say that. Sir." Pushing a finger into the last crumb of crust, Oliver transferred it to his mouth.

"Can you write?"

"Yeah—yes, sir. I could send 'em a letter."

"All right. I'll go down to the office and get some paper and a pencil."

At the sink, Grandma Nellie poured a kettle of steaming water over the stack of dishes.

"Need help?" Oliver asked. "Uh, ma'am?"

When she laughed, her eyes disappeared between round cheeks and dark brows. "What a sweet child! But Mr. Nichols would warm my backside if I put a working boy in an apron. You go get settled in at the desk."

So Oliver crossed the room and pulled an embroidered stool out from under the small rolltop. The same stool lurked in the corner of his parents' living room, though it looked much nicer without that big blue ink stain. He studied its pattern so carefully that Grandma Nellie came over, wiping her hands on a white cloth.

"Isn't that a lovely little seat? It was a wedding present from my parents. My mother said that even a woman living in a boatyard needed a nice place to sit and write." Gathering the papers together that lay on the desk, she folded them into one of the pigeonholes. Oliver climbed up onto the stool and rested his elbows on the dark wood.

Grampa brought back a thick sheet of paper, an envelope with his name and address in the left corner, and a stubby pencil. "You write that letter and address it proper, and Nellie will make sure the mailman picks it up on his rounds tomorrow. There's full letter carrier service here on the island now. Though you probably take that for granted where you live."

"Yes, sir."

Faced with a blank sheet of paper, Oliver's mind blanked to match. He finally settled for the truth: "Dear Mother and Father, I will come home when I can. Don't worry. Your son, Oliver."

Folding the note in half, he slid it into the envelope and turned it over to seal the flap. No stickum—not even the lickable kind.

And what to use for an address? Chewing on the pencil, he wrote: "Mr. and Mrs. John Nichols-Bee, Main Street, Providence Plantations." Hopefully Providence had a Main Street. He certainly couldn't write in his real address, two houses up the hill from where he was now.

"Finished?" Grampa pulled open the top

drawer. "You can use my seal." Lighting a candle stub, he dripped wax onto the back of the envelope and quickly pressed a red stick that looked like a stubby magic marker into the puddle. It left behind a clear imprint: ORN, the initials they shared.

"That's awesome!"

"Mrs. Nichols had it made for me as a wedding present." Grampa fanned the envelope to dry it.

"What'd you give her?"

"That's a rude question." Grampa's cheeks reddened. "I made her a carving."

"An animal?"

"A loon."

"Cause they mate for life."

"How did you know that?"

You taught me, he wanted to say. Instead he shoved fists into his pockets.

Grampa turned. "Nellie Bell, could you make sure John gets this in the morning?" He waved the envelope at her. "Shouldn't let the boy's parents worry." Peering at the address, he nodded. "Nice penmanship. And your name is almost the same as mine. Except for that strange Bee at the end."

Not knowing how to else respond, Oliver faked a yawn.

"Boy's tired, Nell. Where can he sleep?"

"Put our featherbed behind the parlor chairs where it's out of the way. I washed the extra sheet today, so he can use that. And make sure you show him our lovely new bathroom."

Grampa pulled the comforter back from their bed and bundled a thin mattress cover into Oliver's arms. On the small nightstand was a carved loon that would've fit right into his collection at home, and he itched to touch it. Instead he followed his grandfather back to the living room. Together they spread out the featherbed and sheet, adding a tiny pillow stolen from the couch.

He peeled off his seaweedy Sox T-shirt and started to take off his shorts, but the sight of bright blue underwear made him zip up his fly again. Lying under the heavy sheet that smelled like sunshine, Oliver closed his eyes, wondering. Would he wake up back in his own bed and realize it had all been just an awesome dream?

ဢ ဢ ဢ ဢ ဢ

He smelled ashes. Opening his eyes, he spotted the large black woodstove right next to his head. Awesome—he was still in the past! He'd get to spend more time with Grampa, and miss another whole day of school. And maybe he could figure out a way to ask a few questions without freaking anyone out.

"Time to get up, young man."

He sat up and pulled on his smelly T-shirt. Sure was easy to figure out what to wear when you only had one set of clothes.

At the kitchen sink, Oliver watched Grampa brush his teeth with baking soda, the same way he'd done every morning until the day he died. First he dipped a bony finger into the white powder. Then he rubbed it against his teeth, scooped a palmful of water into his mouth, rinsed, and spit.

"Can I try?"

"Sure you can."

Oliver almost gagged, and he had to rinse twice to get rid of the grit, but at least his mouth felt clean again.

Grampa placed a metal coffee pot on the stove and sliced off two generous pieces of the leftover pie. Apple pie for breakfast! Mom definitely wouldn't approve.

"Nellie doesn't like early mornings," Grampa said. "I've learned to fend for myself. Even a perfect wife's gonna do something you don't like."

After pie and coffee (with lots of milk and a heaping spoonful of sugar for Oliver), Grampa led the way downstairs. All of the men were already assembled outside, mumbling to each other, even though it was barely even light out.

"Morning, lads."

"Morning, sir." The four voices sounded a whole lot more eager than Mom's workers.

"I need a crew to rust bust and prep Surprise," Grampa said. "Captain Sam wants her back in the water soon as we can get her painted." He smiled at a thickset teenager. "Eli, she's your favorite. Take Rob and Mason."

"Sure nuf, sir." The kid's blond hair curled into ringlets. "We'll get 'er shined up good. Black again, sir?"

A low chuckle rustled through the group.

"You be tryin' out new paint colors and your backside might be a different color at the end of the day, big as you are," his grandfather growled. "Captain Sam ain't one for surprises, in spite of the boat's name."

"Yes, sir." The kid's grin locked on Oliver, one eye winking closed. Cap'n Eli! Oliver stared after him as he disappeared around the corner into the shed.

Grampa turned to the last worker. "Now John. Soon as Surprise is painted and off the ways we're gonna be hauling boats fast as we

can, so we might as well get some masts out."
He clamped a hand down on Oliver's shoulder.
"You want to teach young Oliver how to pull a
rig the Nichols way?"

"Yes, sir." John's red hair had mostly faded
to silver. He looked a lot older than Grampa
and the rest of the workers.

"Any problems, you find me. I'm taking
care of the lad until his parents come for him."

Three catboats lay alongside floating
timbers that had been cabled together and tied
to the dock. Clambering down the ladder,
John untied the stern line of the first boat.
Oliver followed, uncertain of his footing on the
tar-slippery logs. A silent flick of John's head
indicated the block and tackle dangling from
the top of the tallest piling, so Oliver walked
the bow line forward until the mast lined up
with the derrick.

"Who owns this nice little boat?" Oliver
asked. Wood coamings ran forward to a small
cabin.

"Old man West." John lifted his head

toward the farm across the harbor. The family still owned the property, Oliver remembered. Wonder why they didn't have the same cute catboat?

John tied a line around the varnished mast, hauled the derrick in close, and latched its hook into the loop. Then he circled his finger at Oliver to tension the block and tackle. Oliver pulled the line hand over hand, watching the loop and hook slither up the mast. When John held up a fist Oliver stopped pulling, and John tied off the line.

"Who built her?"

"Hanged if I know." John shrugged. "Seems like every boatbuilder on the Bay has a design that looks like this." Climbing aboard, he untied the mainsheet from the outboard end of the boom.

Oliver stepped onto the foredeck, guessing he'd be needed near the gooseneck. At John's nod he pulled the pin that connected the horizontal boom to the vertical mast, and together they lay the varnished spar down on the deck. He passed a line around it to secure it, and when he looked up John was smiling.

"You're not half as much of a lubber as Mason said."

"Thanks Joh—I mean, sir."

My mom taught me how to unrig boats, he imagined saying. In the twenty-first century. And she learned from the same guy you learned from. So I guess not everything has changed since 1938.

1938—that was the year of the hurricane! They were studying the storm in school for the anniversary. Oliver couldn't remember the exact date. September twenty-something. And today was the fifteenth, according to Grampa's calendar. So they had almost a week to get ready.

But he couldn't help them prepare—it might change the future. He stifled a groan. How could he stand by and watch every boat in the harbor except Surprise be smashed to pieces?

For the first field trip of the school year, his class had gone downtown to see the special

Hurricane of '38 exhibit at the history museum, and one photo had haunted Oliver ever since. Two black automobiles lay on their roofs in the water, and the big white ferry had been speared by the pilings it was supposed to rub against. If the storm had washed heavy cars off the dock and bashed up a huge ship, it was no wonder everything else in the harbor—this catboat and all the skiffs and even the spidery dock—was smashed to kindling. How had Surprise managed to survive?

After pulling the masts out of the other two catboats, Oliver followed John back up to the office, stomach rumbling. Grampa was waiting outside the door, and he reached out to ruffle Oliver's hair. He looked so young! The man he remembered had dark splotches on the back of his hands and wrinkled cheeks. And he'd never seen Grampa bound up a set of stairs so fast.

After another serving of Nellie's stew, Oliver and John climbed into a skiff just like Sparky, towed the three rigless catboats back out to their moorings, and brought two more into the dock to unrig. Even though John was easy to work with, pulling masts sure got old after awhile. No wonder Mom's workers were always complaining.

Just as Oliver's stomach started to growl again, a skinny red-haired boy skipped down the dock. He was maybe ten years old, the same age as Oliver's brother, though he was a whole lot skinnier.

"Hallo, Finn," John said. "How was school?"

"I finished the book."

"You're a reader, just like your mother." John reached up to rumple the bright hair, and Oliver's throat closed. He missed his dad, or anyone he could really talk to without spoiling his own future.

"Oliver, this is my son Finn Murphy. Shake hands, boys." They shook like grownups.

"You want to show him around?" John asked Finn. "I can get this last rig tied up on my own."

"Yeah!" Finn jumped straight up, as if his legs were springs.

"Well, get on then. Oliver's earned a break."

"Awesome! Ah, I mean thanks, sir." Oliver scampered up the ladder after Finn's rolled-up overalls and followed him down to the end of the pier. A railing ran along the edges, and a steel derrick crossed overhead near the ferry slip. Otherwise it was the same old dock he'd played on all his life. As long as he didn't look north and wonder where the bridge was, skipping rocks across the glassy harbor felt almost normal.

Out on Dutch Island, black smoke belched from a ferryboat. "Which one is that?" he asked Finn.

"The good ole Hammonton, running late as usual." Finn rolled his eyes. "I wish they'd build a bridge. But my pa says it would cost too much."

"Why is it late? There's hardly any wind."

"The older ferries break down a lot. And East Ferry always gets the new boats."

"Why?"

"That's the Newport side. Not so much money over here."

Something else that hadn't changed. "What grade are you in?"

"Fourth. But we share a classroom with the stupid third graders. Miss Jonas says the city schools have so many kids there's only one grade in each room." Finn shinnied up one of the tallest bollards and sat down on top. "That true?"

"Yup," said Oliver, throwing a rock as far as he could to watch the distant splash. "Some places even have more than one class in each grade."

"That's grand, a different teacher every year. Pa says I have to stay in until I'm fifteen. You're lucky you got out so young. Or does your family need the money?"

"Yeah." Oliver leaned against the bollard next to Finn's. "Where do you live?"

"Beavertail Road. Just past the big farm, in that little red house on the right."

"Long walk to school."

"I take the bus. There's a bunch of us that live out that way so it's worth it." He pointed to a large, flat rock. "Pass me that one—I want to see if I can skip six from up here."

Several rocks later, John called for Finn and the two boys ran up to the office.

"There you are!" Grampa smiled down at Oliver. "Nice afternoon?"

Oliver stared at his feet, now striped with tar from the bollard he'd tried to climb. "Sorry I left, sir. I–"

"John said you were doing such a great job he forgot how young you were until Finn showed up." Grampa nodded. "I'm glad he let you go early, especially since we haven't talked about wages yet. You might be here until Cap'n Sam can take you back to Providence, and you shouldn't be working for free."

"I don't–"

"Never work for free." His grandfather aimed a finger at Oliver's nose. "If you don't value your own time you'll never value the time of anyone else. I usually start off men with no experience at seventy-five a day. At least until Congress passes that wage law they keep talking about."

"Seventy-five dollars a day?"

"What a jokester you are! I'll pay you on Saturday with the rest of the crew." He bounded upstairs, calling for Nellie.

He must mean seventy-five cents a day. Why even bother?

That evening Oliver pleaded exhaustion and climbed into bed right after dinner, determined to work through everything he could remember about the 1938 hurricane. The dock and the red boatshed would be destroyed, leaving room for the longer dock and taller yellow shed of Oliver's time. Downed trees would take out power for a week. Around the island, people died. And weren't some local kids lost? On a school bus, washed off the causeway while they were trying to get back home to Beavertail....

Finn lived on Beavertail, and he took the bus to school. His new friend was probably going to die in a few days, and he couldn't warn him!

Then again, he couldn't screw up the future by confiding in someone with less than a week to live, could he?

ᕯ ᕯ ᕯ ᕯ ᕯ

A hand shook his bare shoulder.

"Time to get up, boy," Grampa said. "How 'bout oatmeal for breakfast?"

Oliver rubbed the sleep out his eyes. His skin itched. Didn't anybody wash around here? Maybe he could sneak in a swim this afternoon, especially if Finn came by again.

His new friend showed up right after school and taught Oliver how to monkey up onto one of the large bollards. They jumped into the harbor, swam to the ladder, climbed out and dove in again. What fun! When the

Hammonton tooted its arrival, they raced up the pier and scrambled down to the smooth black rocks across from the yard office, where Sparky tied up in Oliver's real life. Finn lay down on his back and closed his eyes, water dripping from his overalls.

Rolling his T-shirt and shorts into a makeshift pillow, Oliver lay down too. The rocks warmed his bare skin, just like the heated seat in his dad's car. And how great was it to swim right off the ferry dock and chase each other between the waiting cars without a single

grownup yelling at them to be careful! He could get used to—

Hearing a sharp intake of breath, he opened his eyes. Finn was staring at his underwear. His bright blue boxers, dotted with yellow comets, orange meteors, and red planets.

"Where'd you get those? They're amazing."

Oliver scrambled to his feet to pull on his shorts. "Can't tell you," he mumbled, zipping up his fly.

"They look like something from the future."

Oliver sat down again, heart pounding.

"Awh, we couldn't afford 'em anyway," Finn said. "We can't even afford regular white undershorts. My pa just started working again a few weeks ago, when Mr. Nichols took on an extra man for hauling season." He turned onto his stomach. "Ma don't like me to tell anyone."

"Listen, Finn. Can you keep a secret?"

"Course I can. Ma threw a surprise thirtieth birthday party for my pa–"

"Your dad's only thirty?" Pasty skin and graying hair made him look more like fifty.

"–I didn't breathe a word about the cake or nothing," Finn finished. "Well a course Ma and my sister Harriet already knew."

"You can't tell this to anyone. Not your mom. Or Harriet. Not that they'd believe you anyway."

"Believe what?"

"Where I come from."

"Huh, I knew you'd made up that guff about Providence! Nobody could stow away on Cap'n Sam's boat without him knowing." Finn rolled onto his side. "So what's the real story?"

"Do you believe in time travel?"

"You mean like Tom Swift and stuff? Gee. I guess so."

"I'm from the future." Oliver plucked the waistband of his underwear. "These are from the next century, from a store almost as big as this island. The man who runs the boatyard, your dad's boss? He's my grandfather."

Two green eyes stared.

"The afternoon I got here, I was skipping school. I'd sneaked aboard Surprise." Oliver shrugged. "I was just gonna hang out, catch a bluefish for dinner, you know? Then I fell down the companionway and hit my head, and the next thing I know Surprise is on the ways and my grampa's yelling at me to get off the boat."

"You do have the same dark hair as Mr. Nichols." Finn frowned. "Why not just tell him?"

"He and Nellie don't even know they're going to have kids yet. I can't just show up and say I'm their grandson."

"Jeepers! I see what you mean. So what do you do now?"

"I've gotta get back to my own time." Oliver wrapped his arms around his bare knees. "I'm just not sure how."

"Wonder what Tom Swift would do."

"I wouldn't know. I haven't read his books."

"But he's the most amazing guy in the whole world! Don't you have enough money for books? Or can't you read?"

"Course I can read. There's just lots of

other things to do in my time."

"Like the radio?" Finn's open mouth revealed crooked bottom teeth. "Radio's neat. My mom won't let me listen to it, except on Sundays."

"Radio's nothing," Oliver said. "But I can't tell you about everything else. It might change the future." He had a sudden fantasy of Finn wearing big silvery headphones, locked in a video game battle with Nat.

"Know any Murphys in your time?" Finn asked.

"There's lots more people on the island. So I wouldn't necessarily—"

"Finn!" John called. "Time to go home."

Scrambling to his feet, Finn hitched up his sagging wet overalls. "I'll read Tom Swift again over the weekend. He's sure to know what you need to do. And I won't tell anyone, I promise." He placed his hand over his heart, underneath the bib of his overalls.

"Thanks, Finn."

As soon as his friend was out of sight, Oliver

stripped off his shorts and hid his underwear beneath a pile of rocks. Better to go without than for someone else to catch a glimpse of the future. He marked the rock pile with a tall stick, making sure no blue showed through. Then he climbed back up the rocks and crossed the pier to the office.

Hopefully Finn wouldn't blab. Though who would believe him anyway? Oliver wasn't sure he believed it himself. Maybe he'd dreamed his whole previous life and had just woken up a few days ago.

But hearing his grandfather's bellow ("Time to go home, Eli! I don't have the money for overtime") told him he had it right. This thirty-year-old man even smelled like sawdust. And Oliver remembered too many details about his own future to think he'd dreamed it all.

"Good time with Finn?" Grampa asked. "He's a nice boy. And maybe Nellie'll have a letter from your parents."

Don't hold your breath, Oliver thought. Wherever Mom and Dad were, it wasn't Main

Street in Providence. Hopefully they weren't going crazy with worry while he figured out how to get himself back to his own time.

Even though the next day was Saturday, Grampa woke him at dawn as usual, and Oliver soon found himself on a tall ladder sanding the transom of Surprise. Mason scraped loose paint off the bulwarks, and Cap'n Eli followed along behind him, puttying the bare spots with a white paste that smelled like old wet shoes.

"I'm taking a certain miss to the theater tonight," Eli said. "You'll never guess who."

"Another new girl?" Mason's long-handled scraper screeched. "You keep going through 'em so fast you'll have to start looking off the island."

"This one's special."

"What's her name?"

"Not telling. You might home in on my girl."

"Hopefully she's too young for me."

"Is her name Pattie?" Oliver asked. "Ouch! Jeez, Eli!" A meaty hand reached around the corner of the transom to slap the back of his head, right on the still tender lump.

"What are you, kid—a mind reader?" Eli's smooth cheeks bloomed red.

"Just a guess," Oliver mumbled.

"I'm takin' her to the second showing of the newsreel," Eli said, loading his knife with another dollop of putty. "I guess that guy Hitler has finally gone too far."

At noon Oliver followed Eli and Mason up to the office, where they lined up to receive their wages.

"Thank you, sir," each man told Grampa.

Oliver received two limp bills. "Thank you, sir," he said, trying to match the men's enthusiasm. He stuffed the bills into the front pocket of his shorts.

"You're a good worker, young man," Grampa replied. "Now, would you like to go to the newsreel this afternoon?"

"Wow, that'd be awesome, Gram—I mean, sir."

His grandfather laughed. "I may seem old

to you, son, but I'm a long way from being a grandfather." He pulled open the outside door. "We can show you our little town. But first of all—my bath!"

b   b   b   b   b

Oliver couldn't remember ever getting excited by an inch of water in a bathtub, steaming as if it had come directly from the kettle—which it had. Without his clothes, Grampa's tan arms and face made it look like he was wearing a white v-neck T-shirt. Scrubbing at his broad chest with a skinny bar of soap, he belted out a song about Nellie Bell, church bells, and cockle shells. Then he popped the drainplug and climbed out, dripping and naked.

As Grampa reached for his clothes, Oliver stripped down to climb in. He turned away when Nellie came in lugging the enormous kettle.

"Nothing I haven't seen before, young Oliver. Now scrub up quick or we'll miss the first show." Her dark hair had been released from its bun and gleamed all the way to her shoulders. She must've bathed before they came home.

Scrubbed clean, with a small rough towel wrapped around his waist, Oliver found a pair of canvas pants and a collarless shirt waiting on top of his bed. Once he'd rolled up the cuffs and added a rope belt, they fit fine. Shoes and underwear? Neither seemed to be required, even for a trip to the theater.

After a quick meal of bread and cheese they strolled up the hill toward town, right past the house where Oliver lived in his normal life. All the windows had been neatly sliced into tiny panes, and white clapboards marched across the front where weathered gray shingles should be.

Grampa smiled up at the pointy roof peak.

"I'd like to own that house someday. But for now our little apartment suits us just fine. Don't you think?" He turned to Nellie, who was all dolled up in a hat, fire-engine-red lipstick, and a blue dress.

"Until we are blessed with children," she replied. "And I pray that will happen soon."

When they met Mason at the four corners where the blinking red traffic light should've been, Oliver hardly recognized him in a clean shirt and slicked back hair. He'd even stuffed his calloused feet into shiny black shoes, though he walked like they pinched.

Nellie took his arm too, and Oliver followed the three grownups over the crest of the hill. East Passage spread out below them like a blue carpet. Though he'd braced himself for the bridgeless Bay, he was still startled by the line of battleships stretching all the way across to Aquidneck Island. His brother would know exactly what kind of ships they were and how many guns and sailors each carried. To Oliver, it was just a wall of gray.

He recognized the theater as the same narrow building where a Chinese takeout and real estate agency would be in his own century. Inside, the wooden seat hit him right on his spine, and the black-and-white newsreel jerked mostly out of focus. And everyone seemed riveted to the pictures of Hitler marching into some country where he didn't belong.

He must have nodded off in the middle, because when his grandfather jabbed him with an elbow the credits were rolling.

"More interested in ice cream, lad?"

"Yes, sir!"

The sun had gone down while they sat inside. Oliver followed Nellie and Grampa down the hill in the golden twilight and they joined a line on the corner, outside a small window. A sign overhead promised candy and ice cream.

Nellie waved up the hill to her left. "They've finished tearing down the Thorndike Hotel. Such a shame; it was a lovely building." Wood boards had been neatly stacked where there would be a bank someday.

"And the Horgan block will be gone next week." Grampa pointed across to a row of empty stores next to the ferry dock. "Lots of changes for our town this year."

You don't know the half of it, Oliver thought.

Grampa bought their ice cream, which only cost a nickel each. They took the cones (vanilla for Grampa and Nellie, chocolate for Oliver) out onto the dock, admiring two large ferries, which did look much newer than the now familiar Hammonton. Glancing back toward the silhouette of downtown, Oliver's mouth dropped open: three shingled buildings with endless porches and cupolas loomed over the waterfront.

"Quite impressive, isn't it," Nellie said. "All those big hotels for the summer people. I was born on this side, but now I like our Dutch Harbor better. Too uppity and crowded over here, especially in the summer."

Still nibbling on his cone, Oliver followed Grampa and Nellie back across the island. Stars were beginning to show up overhead, more than he'd ever seen. Down the west-facing hill, he stopped to admire a treeless view of West Passage. Even in the dark the water shimmered. Three lighthouses blinked: the now familiar white at the south end of Dutch Island, and two lights further south. He recognized Beavertail's sweeping loom, but not the red beam.

"What's that, sir?" Oliver pointed.

"Whale Rock Light. You'll probably meet the keeper tomorrow. He usually comes to Sunday meeting."

The same keeper who'd be lost with his lighthouse in the '38 hurricane? Oliver vowed to avoid him. One almost dead friend was enough.

"Should we take the boy tomorrow, Oliver?" Nellie asked. "I'm sure his parents would appreciate us looking out for his Christian education. And it's the last day the meetinghouse is open this year, so I would like very much to go. But if you don't think it's appropriate–"

"I don't know." His grandfather turned. "What religion were you brought up with, son?"

"None" just didn't seem like a good answer. He remembered his grandfather's memorial service, and the silent dinner grace they'd shared. "Quaker, sir," he replied.

"Perfect!" Nellie clapped her hands around Grampa's elbow. "Would you like to come with us in the morning? I'm sure it's smaller than you're used to, but that doesn't mean you can't know God."

"I guess that's what my parents would want."

"I'm sure of that. If any son of mine was lost, I'd want him taken to meeting."

So the next morning they walked all the way to the meetinghouse up on North Road. The bench was slippery and too tall for Oliver's feet to reach the floor, and only a few people spoke. Mostly it was just silent and really boring. "You were a very good boy," Nellie said as they headed down the hill.

The best part of the whole morning was stopping at the narrow wooden bridge across Zeek's Creek, which Grampa called North Creek since Zeek hadn't been born yet. The tide was falling, and water ripped under the bridge out toward Dutch Harbor. Oliver found a short branch and dropped it in on the up-current side. Then he ran across the dirt lane as fast as he could, just in time to see it spit out under the bridge. Awesome! He'd get run over if he tried that on the fast paved road of his own world.

That afternoon, Grampa listened to the Sox trying to catch the Yankees for the pennant, just like any normal September Sunday. Oliver even recognized a couple of the names— Joe DiMaggio, and Lou Gehrig which he'd thought was a disease.

His grandmother settled into a rocker on the porch with a needle, some yarn, a brown rattle the shape of a potato, and a basket of socks. Oliver sat down on the steps, wishing he could ask about her life. But knowing more of her future than she did wore him out before he'd even opened his mouth, so he stood up again and headed down to the boatyard.

Surprise waited patiently on the ways, her black hull spotty with Eli's putty. Oliver crouched down to toss a few rocks in the water, wishing for Monday. Mom must be completely frantic by now. Maybe they'd given him up for dead already, even had a funeral. Though they must've found Sparky and figured out he'd been on Surprise. He could predict what people would do in his normal world. Here in

1938, things didn't always happen the way he expected.

At least his grandfather hadn't recognized him yet. Grampa only saw what made sense to him, which is why he'd given up going to Sunday meeting after Nellie died. He said her faith was big enough to carry both of them, but without her he just couldn't see what all the fuss was about.

Oliver stared up at Surprise. She looked so young and strong, with varnished masts reaching for the blue sky and fresh sails neatly furled along gleaming booms. He'd wanted to learn more about his grandfather's past, and the towering black schooner had carried him back to her own youth. Now that he wanted to go home again, he just had to trust she would somehow help with that too.

♮   ♮   ♮   ♮   ♮

After a fresh coat of black paint Monday morning, Surprise gleamed. Eli said another coat would go on tomorrow, her bottom would be painted on Wednesday, and Thursday she'd go back in the water. If only Oliver could remember which day the hurricane would hit.

When Finn arrived, panting after the run from school, Oliver scooted over to him and they raced to the end of the pier.

"Have you thought of anything?" Oliver asked.

"I read Tom Swift again yesterday. I told my mom I had a sore throat so I got to stay home from church." A cocky grin showed off his uneven teeth. "You need a portal back to your own time. Which must be Surprise, since she's how you got here."

"That's a no-brain—that's obvious." Oliver stuffed his fists into the still unfamiliar pockets of Grampa's stiff pants. "But I can't just climb aboard and stay there until something happens."

"No you can't—you'd miss supper."

They skipped rocks and talked about their weekend. Finn went on and on about Sunday night's boring radio program, with the same awe in his voice that Nat would use to describe the latest PlayStation game. Oliver kept his eyes on the ground, searching for skipping rocks, only half listening.

Finn spiraled a flat piece of clamshell out across the harbor. "Hey, did you see that? Six skips—that's grand!"

"That's cheating, using a shell."

"It's still six skips."

The most Oliver'd ever skipped was four, but the rocks here seemed easier to hold. Or maybe there were just fewer distractions.

Finn squatted down to inspect a gray stone. "I bet Surprise has to be in the water to be your portal. You'll have to wait till she's launched again."

"But that's three days away! My mom must be freaking out." Oliver scratched his butt, which itched inside the canvas pants. "And I don't know if I can make it through another week without a shower."

"Huh? My dad says it smells like rain. But I don't know what that has to do with time travel."

"Never mind." Oliver rolled his eyes. Finn was on the other side of a cultural gap as wide as the bridgeless Bay.

Tuesday morning, Eli and John brushed a second coat of paint on Surprise's topsides. After lunch, his grandfather stopped outside the office door, nose sniffing the air.

"Smell's like we've got some weather coming."

Oliver inhaled the salty humidity of a stirred up ocean. "What's the date today, sir?"

"The twentieth. Why?"

"Just wondering." September twenty-first, was that the date of the hurricane? He would've paid more attention in class if he'd realized it would have such an impact on his own life.

"You must be counting the days it will take your parents to find you." His grandfather nodded. "They'll send a message as soon as they can. If you got the address right."

Skiffs just like Sparky bumped against the yard pier. Seven more catboats and the gaff-rigged yawl swung on their moorings, still rigged and ready to go sailing.

"Shouldn't we be getting some of these boats out of the water, sir?"

"You sure are a hard worker! But we can't haul anything until we get this old girl back in the drink again." Grampa waved toward Surprise. "So you'll just have to keep your britches on a few more days."

Sniffing the breeze again, his grandfather shook his head. "Weather usually holds till October, anyway."

That night after the lights were turned out, Grampa paced the floor of the bedroom, his awkward gait thumping the floor like a drunken drumbeat. Even without a TV meteorologist to warn him, he could feel something big was on its way.

♭ ♭ ♭ ♭ ♭

The air hovered, heavy and still. Outside the tiny windows, a thin line of smoky clouds raced against gray sky. Today must be it.

Oliver pulled on his filthy shorts and Sox T-shirt, leaving his grampa's clothes on top of the featherbed with the two dollars stuffed into a pocket. After a quick breakfast he followed Grampa down the stairs, but once everyone headed off to work he ran back up to the apartment again to grab the last of Nellie's bread. There was no way to be sure that time travel was always as efficient as—

"Oliver? Is that you?" Nellie came out of the bedroom, pushing a pin into her thick hair.

He held up the crusty heel Grampa had left on the counter. "I was still hungry."

"Growing boy, you are." She reached out to brush his hair out of his eyes.

He started toward the door.

"Wait a minute." She pointed to a familiar envelope lying on the table. "Your parents' letter came back in this morning's post. Are you sure you got the address right?"

"I think so. But I've never written a letter home before."

"Well, don't worry Mr. Oliver about it." Her hand dropped onto the shoulder of his T-shirt. "He didn't sleep very well. We'll sort it out at dinner time."

"Okay." He didn't want her to let go.

"Do you need something else?"

"Guess I'm set now. Bye, Mrs. Nellie."

Her smile warmed him, deep down inside. "Have a good day."

He stared up at her, trying to memorize her face, until her eyebrow V'd into that wave crest just like Mom's. Then after throwing her one last cheeky grin, he pounded down the stairs.

The still harbor reflected dark clouds racing across the sky. Heading straight for Surprise, Oliver climbed aboard to stash the bread in the galley sink. Hopefully it wouldn't get wet before he could eat it. Too bad he didn't have a Ziploc—

"That must be young Oliver." A voice rumbled from behind the engine.

"Jeez, Eli! You made me jump." His heels backed into something hard.

An open-topped carryall squatted behind him on the cabin sole. The one he'd whacked his head on, back in his other life.

"This your toolbox?"

"Sure 'nuf. I built it when I started working here last year."

"Why'd you leave it in the middle of the cabin? I keep tripping over it."

"So it's handy. That ducky's hard to move." Eli pointed to the row of empty holes running down one side. "It looks too big now, but I'll fill it up by and by. I buy a new tool every time I get some extra cash." He lifted his gaze from the freshly varnished box. "Aren't you supposed to be tying up those rigs with John?"

"I just wanted to make sure Surprise was okay."

"You sure got a thing for this boat. Me too. Right beauty she is, and she sails like a wet hen." He thumped the top of the engine. "No thanks to this old clunker. Boss asked me to tune her up, but I'd rather toss her over the side. Once you get into trouble, an engine don't–"

"Oliver!" His grandfather shouted. "You up there again?"

"Criminy." Eli shook his head. "Old man's got ants in his pants. Been prowling around ever since we started, yelling at anything that moves. Better jump to it." Reaching across the engine, he opened up an oily rag to reveal a metal disc the size of a small roll of tape. "And scare me up some screws for this oil pump cover, would you? Old ones 're stripped."

Sliding the cover into the side pocket of his shorts, Oliver scrambled up the ladder and down the ways as fast as he could.

Grampa's arms were crossed, and black eyebrows had merged into one jagged line. Oliver smiled up at him. "I thought Eli might need help."

"Eli needs to be left alone so he can get that mother of an engine tuned up."

"Yes, sir. And don't you think you'd better be...." His voice trailed off.

"Better be what? What are you trying to say?"

Oliver looked down at his feet. "I don't feel quite right."

Grampa laid a heavy hand on his shoulder. "Go on upstairs and get Nellie to make you some chamomile tea. Settle your stomach." Dark eyes lifted to the racing clouds. "I might be up for some myself in a bit. I don't feel quite right either."

When Grampa's gaze turned back to the harbor, Oliver detoured into the shed and hid behind a large stack of planks. He wanted to be with his grandfather, but he'd only get in the way or say something stupid.

Feet shuffled in and out through the doorway. The sky was darkening, and a thick patter of raindrops began on the shed roof and then stopped. In the sudden quiet, Grampa's voice carried easily.

"Mason! Tell Eli to run some extra lines on Surprise and get down off her. It's coming on to blow, and I think it might be bad."

Someone had slid the shed doors almost closed to keep out the rain, so Oliver crawled out of his hiding place to peek through the gap. Eli tied lines to Surprise's two stern cleats and threw them down to Mason, who hitched them to the ways. Two lines were passed down from the bow as well. The schooner towered over everyone, well above the high water mark on the beach below, and Oliver could see Mason shaking his head as if questioning Grampa's sanity. Now it was obvious why Surprise was the only boat in the harbor to survive the storm.

The rain started its patter again, forcing the men into the shed. Eli made a lame joke about standing around on the old man's time (Nichols' nickel), but instead of finishing it off with his customary wink, his eyes darted back out toward the harbor. Peering up into the now familiar young face, Oliver wished he could warn him to get out and go home, before this flimsy shed collapsed.

The last one to come inside was Grampa. Hovering just inside the doors, he stared out into the downpour, water running off his hair onto crossed arms.

Oliver tried to etch the smooth cheeks into memory. Getting to know Grampa as he was in the past had showed Oliver what he really wanted: more time together in the future, more carved animals, more time to be a grandson. Wasn't there some way to bring him back home? Angling his head toward the tan work shirt, Oliver inhaled the sawdust scent, the unsaid goodbye forming a lump in his throat.

When the first flash of lightning blinded everyone, Oliver dodged out through the crack in the doors and scurried across the yard.

"Get back in here!"

Even though tide was an hour past high, the water was coming up so fast the big schooner had already started to shift on the ways. An eerie moan of wind drove needles of rain into his face, forcing him to squint. He almost lost his footing scrambling up the slippery oak beams, and his T-shirt caught in a loose strand of wire as he slid over the lifeline. Ripping it free, he collapsed in a heap on the cockpit seat, breathing hard. He wanted to take a last look around, but he couldn't see past the rain and he could hardly stand against the building breeze.

Bye, Finn. Bye, Grandma Nellie. Bye—

"Oliver! Get down right now!" Grampa was on the ground below. He had to hurry.

He slid the smooth hatch forward, releasing a whiff of gasoline. Eli must've been cleaning the filter. Finding the top step with one wet foot, Oliver scrambled down into the fumes. The wind had built out of nowhere and now it howled in the rigging, shaking the whole schooner and blowing rain down into the sink. Luckily the heel of bread still felt dry. Just as he took a bite, a wave caught Surprise under the stern counter, lurching her forward. Stumbling once again over Eli's stupid toolbox, the last thing he saw was a streak of lightning through the open hatch.

♭ ♭ ♭ ♭ ♭

When Oliver swam back to consciousness, a familiar face came into focus.

"Mom?" he rasped. His throat felt raw, as if he had swallowed the gasoline instead of just inhaling it.

"He's awake! Peter, he's said something!" His mother's dark hair was matted, and her sweatshirt looked slept in. Like she hadn't washed more than once in the past week, just like him.

"Where am I?"

"The hospital. You've been here six days. Ever since we discovered you on Surprise." She smoothed the hair out of his eyes.

"Where does it hurt?" Dad pushed up against the opposite side of the bed. "Can you move your toes?"

He did a mental check through his body. "Nothing hurts, and everything moves. What am I doing here?"

"You've been in a coma, and you had a high fever the past twelve hours." Dad's cool hand felt his forehead. "Now your temp's normal. That's amazing."

"I feel fine. Just tired. And hungry."

The room echoed with his family's laughter. Nat even smiled across a lapful of shiny DVD player.

"Sorry I worried you," Oliver told his mom.

"Your mom wasn't as worried as I was," Dad replied.

Mom leaned down to whisper into Oliver's right ear. "That's because I was sitting here the first night, holding your hand, and I saw Grampa. He told me you were on an adventure and you'd be back in a few days. I'd never dreamed about him before, but I knew he wouldn't tell me something that wasn't–"

"Figures you'd wake up during a storm," Nat said, eyes back on his movie.

"What storm?"

"Tropical Storm Finn," Mom said. "It's been blowing dogs off chains all day."

"Will Sparky be okay?"

"She'll be fine—we pulled her up on the pier and turned her upside down." The color washed out of Mom's face. "Thank goodness you'd tied her alongside Surprise. We might not have found you in time."

"They're calling this the anniversary storm," Dad said. "Because of–"

"The '38 hurricane," Oliver finished. Both his parents stared down at him. "We're studying it in school," he said, the heat rising to his cheeks.

"Nice to know something sunk in," Dad said. "Ms. Marshall said you've been pretty distracted."

"She came to see you yesterday," Mom added. "Said not to worry about making up your schoolwork."

"How's Cap'n Eli?"

"About the same, unfortunately."

"I guess he must be kinda mad. About my being on Surprise and all."

"He'll be happy to hear you woke up." His father reached out a closed fist. "But you should return what was in your pocket."

A five-cornered piece of metal dropped into Oliver's palm—the oil pump cover Eli had given him, just before the storm.

"Cap'n Eli wouldn't mind you visiting Surprise," his mother said. "But he certainly wouldn't appreciate you taking things."

"But he gave it to me—"

"The old engine piece he'd mounted on the bulkhead of Surprise?" Mom shook her head. "He'd never part with that. You'll have to give it back." And then her left eyebrow crested into that wave, just exactly like Grandma Nellie's. "Understand?"

Mom had round cheeks, too.

"Oliver?"

He lowered his chin. "Okay, I promise."

"You can deliver it yourself when you're up to it. He's right down the hall. I'm sure he'd love to hear all about your adventure on Surprise."

"We gotta save her, Mom. She was really cool when she was new. I mean, that's what Grampa always said. I've been thinking about her a lot. Dreaming, maybe." He felt his face growing hot. "She can't just rot away once Eli's gone. I've got that money I saved from–"

"Cap'n Eli's daughter found a buyer, honey. He's the grandson of the very first owner. Eli says now he can die happy."

"Wow that's grand. I mean, awesome!"

Mom chuckled. "What were you dreaming about, anyway? You kept mumbling something about six skips."

Clutching the oil pump cover so hard it dug into his palm, Oliver tried to wink up at her like Cap'n Eli would have. "I can't tell you exactly—it's all a little fuzzy. But Grampa says hi."

ABOUT THE HURRICANE

୨ ୨ ୨ ୨ ୨

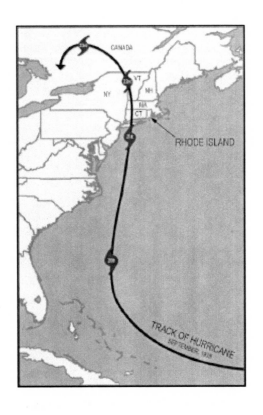

The Great Hurricane that hit New England on
September 21, 1938 was the first major hurricane
to strike the area in almost seventy years. Unlike
modern storms, there was little or no warning of
its arrival. Five hundred people lost their lives
and thousands of boats, businesses, and homes

were damaged. Seventy years later, the Storm of '38 still provides a weather benchmark along the Rhode Island and Connecticut shorelines, and its memory lives on even in the landlocked states of New England that felt its wrath.

When the hurricane made landfall on Long

Photo courtesy Jamestown Historical Society

Island, New York, it was strong, fast-moving, and Category 3, which means it had sustained winds above 110 miles per hour. To make matters worse, just a few short hours remained before high tide. Speeding across Long Island Sound, the intense weather system downed trees and power lines in Connecticut, Rhode Island, Massachusetts, sped north into New Hampshire and Vermont, and finally broke up over Canada.

September 21st was both the autumnal equinox and a full moon. As a result, the tide was already much higher than usual when the storm hit. In Narragansett Bay, the storm surge was funneled by the Bay's shape and water rose to a level of nearly sixteen feet above normal. At the top corner of the Bay, street flooding in Providence submerged rush hour cars and trolleys. People were trapped on the upper floors of office buildings, watching as water swirled up the streets below.

On the island where Oliver lives, seven children died when their school bus tried to cross a narrow causeway and the bus stalled in the waves washing across the road. These brave children left the bus,

Photo courtesy Dutch Island Lighthouse Society

attempting to form a human chain to safety, but the raging waters were too strong. All but one of the children were swept away.

A few miles to the southwest, Whale Rock lighthouse was washed off its base by the pounding waves. The lighthouse was over a hundred years old. The keeper's body was never found.

The hurricane's destruction of the ferry docks on either side of West Passage broke down all local

Photo courtesy Jamestown Historical Society

opposition to building a bridge across the Bay, and less than two years after the hurricane, the span that Finn had dreamed of opened for travel.

ϑ ϑ ϑ ϑ ϑ

ABOUT THE SCHOONERS

♪ ♪ ♪ ♪ ♪

*Chesapeake oystering. Charles E. Emery collection,
Annapolis Collection Gallery.*

Most of the ships that we now think of as tourist
attractions were built to carry cargo. Just as we take
little notice of the trucks crowding our towns and
highways, working schooners like Surprise never

attracted much attention during the sixty years they sailed in and out of U.S. harbors. Like our clunky delivery vans and tractor trailers, yesterday's hard-working schooners were just doing their job.

From the mid-1800's until about 1930, thousands of "coasters" sailed along the shorelines of the United States, moving everything from building materials like lumber and coal to luxuries like oysters and Long Island duck. It is hard to overstate their importance to trade and development, especially where cities had been built alongside large estuaries (San Francisco, Baltimore, Providence) or lakes (Chicago, Detroit, Cleveland). Roads were seldom paved and interstates did not yet exist, so overland transportation was expensive and slow compared to moving cargo by water. Coasters were what knitted these urban centers together, forging a national identity that otherwise would have taken much longer to develop.

The classic schooner sailplan (two masts, with the forward one slightly shorter) was so popular because each sail was a manageable size. Schooners were also nimble enough to enter and leave small harbors in most weather. Hull shapes maximized cargo capacity and minimized draft (the nautical term for how deep a boat sits in the water). Many ships were built with centerboards, which were swing keels that could be raised when creeping into shallow harbors and lowered in deeper water to improve sailing ability.

Smaller coasters like Surprise were traditionally run by "two men and a boy," and one of the men was usually the owner. The skipper was usually called "Cap'n Eli" (or whatever his first name was) and he pitched in to help make sail or unload cargo.

Schooner ALICE S. WENTWORTH off Cape Poge, MA.
©Mystic Seaport, Photography Collection, Mystic, CT

A few wives joined their skipper husbands onboard as cooks and also helped run the vessels.

What did coasters carry, and where did they go? The answers are as varied as the coastline. On the East Coast, one common round trip was to bring lime, stone, or ice from Portland, Maine down to New York City and then return with coal. On the West Coast, hardwoods sailed from the Northwest forests down to rapidly expanding cities like San Francisco (especially after the devastating fire of 1905). In the Gulf of Mexico, coasters unloaded oysters from larger schooners anchored offshore and sailed them across the shallows into market. To the north, grain moved from prairie to city by Great Lakes schooner. Fresh water vessels also transported furs from remote trading posts south to Chicago and other major cities.

On every coast, lumber (which seemed to include anything made of wood) was a popular cargo. Its advantage was obvious once a coaster started to sink. Many schooners made it into their last port "on their cargo," afloat only because of the positive buoyancy of the wood in their holds.

And as cities developed, the demand for lumber increased the demand for shipping—which increased the demand for lumber to build more ships. Stacks often extended beyond the ship's rails, so high that skippers had to stand on top of their load to see forward.

Other bulk cargoes included coal, grain, salt, ice, lime, granite, and paving stone. As demand for such goods increased, so did the size of the schooners—and the number of masts on which the sails were set. Three-masters became a common sight between Maine and New York or Seattle and San Francisco. Several four, five, and even six-masters were built, though only one seven-master was ever completed.

Smaller coasters carried more specialized items over shorter distances. Brick, clay, sand, road oil, cotton, potatoes—everything that was needed to build small towns and expand large cities—was carried by schooner.

Although most coasters delivered whatever paid best, the Key West schooner Western Union carried the same unique cargo for thirty-five years.

California's three-masted C.A. Thayer in her cod-fishing days. Courtesy San Francisco Maritime NHP.

Built in 1939, this 130-foot vessel maintained undersea telegraph cables between Key West, Cuba, and the Caribbean. The schooner still daysails out of Key West and is on the National Register of Historic Places.

Once shorelines had been cleared of lumber and motor-driven vessels grew large and dependable enough to carry bulk cargoes, the sailing schooner's era quickly came to an end. By the 1920's, tugs

*The schooner Westerm Union, now carrying
passengers for hire out of Key West, FL.*

pulling coal barges (similar to the ones in use today) had established a reliability that wind-driven coasters could never match. Other long distance cargoes were gradually taken over by steamers, as well as by shore-based transportation systems like railroads and trucks. While coasters continued to make local deliveries, especially in the San Francisco and Chesapeake Bays and among the many islands of the Maine coast, only a handful of schooners nationwide lived to see World War II. An even smaller number survives today, beautiful reminders of the glorious days of transportation by sail.

Additional Information

1. <u>Zeb: Celebrated Schooner Captain of Martha's Vineyard</u>, by Polly Burroughs; Insider's Guide, 2005.

2. <u>Wake of the Coasters</u>, by John F. Leavitt, Marine Historical Association, Inc., 1970.

3. <u>Schooners in Four Centuries</u>, by David R. MacGregor, Naval Institute Press, 1982.

4. Maine Windjammer Association, www.sailmainecoast.com

5. Schooner Western Union Maritime Museum, www.schoonerwesternunion.com

6. San Francisco Maritime Park, http://www.nps.gov/safr/historyculture/historic-vessels.htm

⚓ ⚓ ⚓ ⚓ ⚓

GLOSSARY

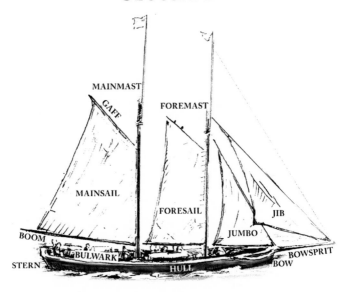

BLOCKING   A solid piece of wood used to support a boat set down on the ground.

BOAT STAND   A three-legged metal support with a flat wood top, used in pairs under a hauled out boat to keep her upright.

BOLLARD   A wooden post on a pier to which mooring lines are tied.

BOOM   A long spar used to extend the bottom edge of a sail.

BOOTLEGGING   To manufacture or carry alcoholic beverages illegally.

BOTTOM PAINT	A special coating applied to boat bottoms to reduce marine growth.
BOW	The forward part of a boat.
BULKHEAD	A partition separating a boat into cabins that also provides structural integrity.
BULWARK	The side of a ship above the upper deck.
CABIN SOLE	The collection of floorboards used to cover over the deep interior or bilge of a boat.
CARRYALL	A toolbox, usually wooden, with an open top.
CATBOAT	A sailboat with a single mast far forward. Commonly sailed around New England as both a pleasure boat and workboat.
CAULKING	Material used to fill gaps between the planks in a boat's hull, in order to make the hull watertight.
CLEAT	A fitting with two projecting horns around which a rope may be made fast.
COAMING	A raised frame around a hatch or deck area designed to keep water out.
COASTER	A ship sailing along a coast, usually engaged in trade.

GLOSSARY, *continued*

COCKPIT
: An enclosed area from which a boat is steered.

COMPANIONWAY
: A ship's stairway from one deck to another.

DERRICK
: A tall pole with a rope and pulley system at the top, which provides mechanical advantage for hoisting.

FOREDECK
: The forward part of a ship's main deck.

FORESAIL
: A square sail set on the foremast, the next mast forward of the mainmast.

GAFF-RIGGED
: Any ship that has a sail with a gaff, a horizontal pole which supports the upper edge of a four-sided sail.

GOOSENECK
: The fitting on the mast where the boom attaches.

HYDRAULIC TRAILER
: A u-shaped frame used to haul and launch boats. Padded arms can be adjusted to fit against the hull for support during transport.

INBOARD
: Toward the centerline of a ship.

JIB
: A triangular sail that extends from the top of the mast to the bow.

JUMBO
: A triangular sail that sets just forward of the foremast.

LIFELINE	A wire running forward from the bulwarks that prevents people from falling overboard.
LOBSTER BUOY	A small color-coded float that marks the location of a lobster trap on the bottom.
LOWERS	The four lowest sails on a schooner, which are easily set and managed by a small crew.
LUBBER	A big clumsy fellow. (Used here as short for landlubber, or non-sailor.)
MAINSAIL	The principal sail set on the mainmast.
MAINSHEET	A rope that trims and secures the mainsail.
MAST	A long pole or spar rising from the keel or deck of a boat.
PLANKING	Wood boards lined up on edge that make up a ship's hull
PORT	The left side of a boat when looking forward.
PORTAL	A door or entrance (here used to travel through time).
PRESSURE WASHER	A pump that sprays water at very high pressure, used for cleaning.

GLOSSARY, *continued*

PULL A RIG	To remove a mast from a boat, usually with a crane or derrick.
ROLLTOP DESK	An old-fashioned piece of furniture consisting of a writing desk with a cover that slides down over it.
RUST BUST	To remove rust stains from a hull, in preparation for painting.
SCAFFOLD	A temporary platform when working at a height above ground.
SCHOONER	A ship with more than one mast and the largest sail aft, commonly used for carrying cargo along the coast and overseas. Most schooners still in use today take passengers for tours.
SHIP OARS	To pull oars into the boat and stow them, usually under the thwart.
SKIFF	A light rowboat.
SPAR	A stout rounded wood pole used to support rigging.
STARBOARD	The right side of a boat when looking forward.
STAYSAIL	A sail set forward of the mainmast.
STERN	The rear end of a boat.
THWART	A seat extending across a boat.

TOPSIDES	The outer surface of a boat above the waterline.
TRANSOM	The planking that forms the stern of a square-ended boat.
TRAWL	A large frame that drags a net along the sea bottom to gather fish.
WATERLINE	The line marked on a boat that corresponds with the surface of the water.
WAYS	A permanent structure used to haul or launch a boat.
YAWL	A sailboat with the smaller sail closer to the stern.

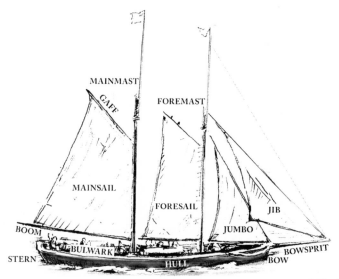

About the Author

Carol Newman Cronin has sailed and written fiction since she was a child. In 2004, she crowned a lifetime of competitive achievement by winning two races for the USA at the Olympics in Athens. A member of the elite US Sailing Team from 2001–2007, she has won numerous national and international sailing championships. Since retiring from Olympic sailing, Carol has focused on writing and graphic design from her home office in Jamestown, RI. She and her husband spend as many hours as possible on the water, mostly aboard a Herreshoff Marlin that was built in 1938.

About the Illustrator

Laurie Ann Cronin grew up on the Hudson River, sailing an old wooden family-owned nineteen foot Rocket that sealed a lifelong love of the water. A graduate of Syracuse University with a degree in painting, Laurie is currently an Art Director/Designer and lives with her husband and son. She visits the water as often as possible, on the nearby Finger Lakes or farther afield in the salty waters of Narragansett Bay.

OLIVER'S NEXT ADVENTURE...

He vowed he would stay in his own time, but when bad clams meet bad weather all bets are off. Oliver's next adventure takes him and Surprise east to Cape Cod, where he finally meets his crazy aunt Liza. And in order to get back to the present he might have to use what he learned during the Hurricane of '38...

AVAILABLE IN 2010

Breinigsville, PA USA
15 September 2010
245454BV00001B/1/P